FORGED ON
FREEDOM
THE MAKING OF AMERICA

The
CONSTITUTION
Defender of Freedom

Amie Jane Leavitt

PURPLE TOAD
PUBLISHING

P.O. Box 631
Kennett Square, Pennsylvania 19348
www.purpletoadpublishing.com

FORGED ON
FREEDOM
THE MAKING OF AMERICA

The Constitution: Defender of Freedom
The Amendments: Protector of Freedom
The Revolutionary War: The War for Freedom
Roots of the Revolution

PUBLISHER'S NOTE: The data in this book has been
researched in depth, and to the best of our knowledge
is factual. Although every measure is taken to give an
accurate account, Purple Toad Publishing makes no
warranty of the accuracy of the information and is not
liable for damages caused by inaccuracies.

Printing 1 2 3 4 5 6 7 8 9

Publisher's Cataloging-in-Publication Data
Leavitt, Amie Jane
 The Constitution : defender of freedom / Amie Jane
Leavitt
   p. cm. – (Forged on freedom. The making of
America)
Includes bibliographic references and index.
ISBN: 978-1-62469-006-8 (library bound)
1. United States. Constitution – Juvenile literature. 2.
United States – Politics and government – 1775–1783 –
Juvenile literature.   I. Title.
 E303.L43 2013
 342.7302'9—dc23
                                                    2013930980

eBook ISBN: 978-1-62469-017-4

Printed by Lake Book Manufacturing, Chicago, IL

CONTENTS

Chapter One: A Nation in Crisis 4
    The Articles of Confederation 11

Chapter Two: Creating a More Perfect Union 12
    The Delegates Arrive 19

Chapter Three: A Hot and Muggy Summer............20
    Franklin's Plea 27

Chapter Four: The Value of Compromise 28
    Slavery and the Constitution.............................33

Chapter Five: Off to the States................................34
    A Rising Sun 41

Timeline...42

Chapter Notes 43

Further Reading...45

    Books 45

    Works Consulted...45

    On the Internet 45

Glossary...46

Index..47

A Nation in
CRISIS

On January 25, 1787, snow—four feet high—towered on the farmlands and country roads like a thick fortress wall. Dew froze in long icy daggers on skeletal tree limbs. Daniel Shays and his group of Regulators trudged through this forbidding landscape toward the arsenal at Springfield, Massachusetts. The buildings there housed valuable munitions owned by the United States government. Not only did the Regulators need the arsenal's cannons, muskets, barrels of gunpowder, and other weaponry, they also hoped to find refuge from the bitter cold. Many of the 1,500 Regulators were braving the frigid New England winter in thin coats or no coats at all. The locals reported that this was the coldest winter they had experienced in many, many years.[1]

Daniel Shays was not new to the miserable conditions of military life. He had fought valiantly as a captain in the Revolutionary War in such battles as Bunker Hill, Ticonderoga, Saratoga, and Stony Point.[2] Yet the Revolutionary War was long over. In fact, the British had surrendered at Yorktown more than six years before, in October 1781. So these men weren't seeking the arsenal's weaponry to fight the British. In an odd turn of events

The Regulators pushed forward toward the arsenal, assuming that the soldiers who were guarding the building would not fire upon them. They were wrong.

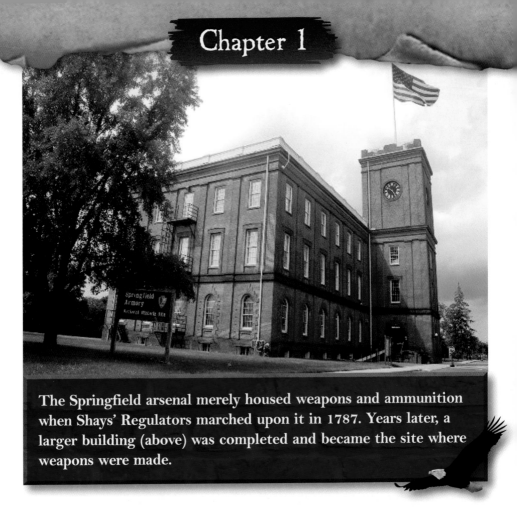

The Springfield arsenal merely housed weapons and ammunition when Shays' Regulators marched upon it in 1787. Years later, a larger building (above) was completed and became the site where weapons were made.

Shays and his men—many of whom were Patriot soldiers too—were now rebelling against the very United States government that they had fought so hard to establish.[3]

Why?

For years now, Revolutionary War veterans had been begging the United States government to give them their paychecks—many of which were *long* overdue. But the government was broke. It had no money to pay the veterans for their service during the war. In fact, the government had no money to pay anyone, not even the other countries that had helped the Patriots during the war. The government had no way to make money, either. The Articles of Confederation—the document that organized the thirteen states during the Revolutionary War—prohibited Congress from taxing the people. Without any way to bring in money, the government could not pay its debts. In the end, it was the people who really suffered.[4]

When the veterans didn't receive their pay, they couldn't pay the loans on their homes and farms. They couldn't pay businesses that had sold them goods and supplies. It wasn't just the veterans who suffered. Many Americans were experiencing tough economic times. Back in the 1700s, it was considered a serious crime not to pay your debts, serious enough that you could be sent to debtors' court. A judge would order you to sell your home, farm, and business. If this income wasn't enough to pay what you owed, you'd be arrested and locked away in debtors' prison.[5]

Daniel Shays and some of his fellow farmers in Western Massachusetts were tired of watching their friends and families lose everything in debtors' court. After all, they had not fought for freedom from the British only to lose everything they owned and spend the rest of their days rotting away in prison. This wasn't the kind of "liberty" they had imagined when they had fought the war for independence.

In the fall of 1786, Shays and a group of like-minded men dressed in their Revolutionary War uniforms and marched to their local courthouse.

When the rebellion started in 1786, Daniel Shays was 39 years old. He was a farmer who worked about 100 acres of land in Pelham, Massachusetts. After the events on January 25, 1787, Shays fled to Vermont. He was condemned to death by Massachusetts authorities, but was later pardoned by the state's governor, John Hancock.

They stood outside the courthouse armed with muskets, clubs, swords, and even pitchforks. When the judges and lawyers arrived for work, Shays' men would not let them into the building. Their idea was simple: if the judges and lawyers could not get into the courthouse, then court could not be held. If court could not be held, then people who were in financial trouble would not lose their property and go to jail. Shays and his men weren't the only people in the Regulators group. Other groups from all across Western Massachusetts marched on their local courthouses, too.[6]

Not everyone agreed with the Regulators' ideas, though. Some felt that it wasn't right to take the law into one's own hands. They didn't

All was not peaceful after the Americans won their freedom from British rule. The young nation struggled greatly under the Articles of Confederation. A new framework was desperately needed.

want to live in a place where anyone at any time could take up arms and force the government to change the way it operated. This wasn't the kind of America the people had signed up for either.[7]

In January 1787, groups of Regulators in Western Massachusetts had decided to band together. They wanted to march to Boston and force the state government to help people who were struggling financially. But before they could go, they needed to obtain weapons. And that was the goal of this stop in Springfield.[8]

As the Regulators continued their march toward the arsenal on this wintry January day, they spied a group of state militia guarding the front of the building. The militia saw them too.

The militia's leader, General William Shepard, shouted a warning that the men had three minutes to disperse peaceably.

The Regulators kept marching forward.

General Shepard ordered his men to fire. Cannonballs rocketed high above the Regulators' heads and into the nearby pine forest.

The Regulator leaders really didn't believe that the militia would do more than fire these warning shots. They ordered the men to keep marching forward.

But the militia really did mean business. The next round of cannonballs tore right through the front line of Regulators at waist height, killing four men and wounding dozens of others.

Chaos broke out. Shays and the other Regulator leaders tried to keep the men organized, but it was no use. The younger men, who had never experienced battle before, were terrified and fled into the woods. With the small number of men who were left, the leaders had no choice but to retreat.[9]

And so it was that January 25, 1787, landed its place in United States history. From the point of view of Shays and his Regulators, the day had been an utter disaster. From the point of view of the state militia, it had been a tremendous success. From the point of view of the rest of the country, it was a key moment that pushed the government in a new direction. The new nation was in crisis, and if it were not addressed soon, everything that had been won during the Revolutionary War would vanish.[10]

But what could be done to help the country?

Some of the Revolutionary War leaders, including James Madison and Alexander Hamilton, had been worried about the country for quite some time.[11] Just about every state in the Union was experiencing some sort of problem. The outbreaks in Massachusetts, especially Shays' Rebellion, seemed to be the tipping point. The Revolutionary leaders started looking for the root of the problem. Madison and Hamilton, and others with their same views, believed that the nation's problems stemmed from the Articles of Confederation. George Washington was one of these leaders. He believed that the strong state governments created under the Articles of Confederation would eventually ruin the United States as a whole. He stated, "Thirteen sovereignties [states] pulling against each other, and all tugging at the federal head [government], will soon bring ruin on the whole."[12] The national government had to be strengthened. If it weren't, then, he claimed, "like a house on fire, whilst the most regular form of extinguishing it is contended for, the building [will be] reduced to ashes."[13]

The way the central government was set up under the Articles of Confederation became enough of a concern that Congress called a special session for May 1787. Each state was to send delegates to Philadelphia for the Federal Convention, which was also known as the Constitutional Convention. They would meet in the Pennsylvania State House, the same place that the Declaration of Independence had been signed only eleven years before. The purpose of the meeting was to revise the Articles of Confederation. Every state except Rhode Island sent delegates to the convention. This tiny state was so concerned about losing its states' rights and being overrun by the larger states that it refused to participate.[14]

The Articles
of Confederation

The Articles of Confederation was a document that had been accepted by the states in March 1781, just seven months before the end of the Revolutionary War. Many of the people in the United States were opposed to a strong central government. After all, they felt that this is what had caused all of their problems with the British. The Articles of Confederation was designed to protect state governments and keep them independent. The document was basically just a bond of friendship between the states. The state governments had rights to do just about anything they wanted. They could print their own currency. They could make treaties with other nations. They could regard or disregard treaties made by Congress. They could form their own navies. They could refuse to trade with other states or nations, or charge excessive fees for goods from certain places and not from others.

On the other hand, under the Articles of Confederation, the federal government, called the Confederation Congress, was pretty much powerless. Congress could not tax the people. It could not make rules and decisions about trade. It could not settle arguments between the states or protect the country from foreign invaders. Every decision that Congress made had to be approved unanimously by the states, which meant that anything proposed by Congress was rarely passed. Under the Articles of Confederation, the states functioned as if they were their own individual countries, not members of one united country.[15]

Cover of the
Articles of
Confederation

Chapter 2

Creating a More
PERFECT UNION

On May 25, four months to the day after the bloody encounter in Massachusetts between the Regulators and the militia, a group of men peacefully assembled in Philadelphia.

The sky wasn't blue that first morning of the convention. In fact, rain poured down in a steady stream from heavy, gray clouds.[1] Guards stood at the entrance to the Pennsylvania State House and allowed only the invited delegates inside.[2] One by one, horse-drawn carriages pulled up to the building's main doors, and from them climbed such notable figures as George Washington of Virginia, Gouverneur Morris of Pennsylvania, Luther Martin of Maryland, and Elbridge Gerry of Massachusetts. Of course, Madison and Hamilton came, too, representing their states of Virginia and New York, respectively. Eighty-one-year-old Pennsylvanian Benjamin Franklin, the oldest delegate to the convention, was suffering from the crippling effects of gout and was not present on this day.[3] Many of the onlookers were probably surprised

Benjamin Franklin (far right) had many visitors at his home during the Federal Convention, including (left to right) Alexander Hamilton, James Madison, and James Wilson.

The Pennsylvania State House where the Declaration of Independence and the Constitution were written and signed. Today, it is called Independence Hall.

that they did not see John Adams and Thomas Jefferson, either—after all, both men had played such important roles in the writing of the Declaration of Independence. But Adams and Jefferson were serving overseas as ambassadors to Great Britain and France at the time and were thus unable to attend the convention.[4]

Once the men were all inside the statehouse and the main doors were closed, workers quickly began shoveling dirt from wooden carts and smoothing it over the cobblestone streets surrounding the building. The dirt would muffle the clickety-clack of passing horses, carriages, and carts. The delegates would need all the peace and quiet they could get in order to focus on the important matters at hand.[5]

Inside the statehouse, the delegates made their way into the Assembly Room. Most of the men in attendance were very familiar with this place. After all, right there in 1775, the Continental Congress had chosen George Washington to be the Continental Army's commander in chief.[6] At these very same green-cloth-covered tables in 1776, members of the Continental Congress risked their lives and fortunes when they signed the Declaration of Independence.[7] In 1777, America's first flag of stars and stripes was chosen there.[8] And in 1781, near the end of the war, the Articles of Confederation were approved.[9] Of all the men in attendance, eight were signers of the Declaration of Independence, fifteen had helped work on their own state constitutions, and twenty-five had served in the Continental Congress during the Revolutionary War.[10]

Once the delegates were seated in their specified areas organized by state,[11] Robert Morris, who had been one of the financiers of the Revolutionary War, made his way to the front of the room. He explained that since the convention was being held in Pennsylvania, he—as a delegate from Pennsylvania—would open the proceedings. The first order of business was for the men to choose a president for the convention.

"I nominate George Washington, our previous commander in chief," he firmly stated.[12]

John Rutledge of South Carolina seconded the motion, and all the delegates voted in favor.[13] This vote would be one of the only times during the four-month convention that the delegates would agree upon anything unanimously.

Washington stood and addressed his fellow delegates—many of whom he considered friends. In his typical gracious style, he thanked them for their confidence in him. He humbly informed them that although he didn't feel adequately qualified, he would do his best to fulfill his responsibilities as the convention's president.[14]

On the next day of the convention, which was Monday, May 28, the delegates agreed on a set of rules. The most important was that each state—regardless of size or number of delegates—would be allowed one vote on issues discussed at the convention. In order for something to be passed, only a majority of votes was needed—not the unanimous votes that had been required in the Articles of Confederation.[15]

The real debates of the convention began on Tuesday, May 29. On this day Edmund J. Randolph, the governor of Virginia, presented a plan that he and the other delegates from Virginia had been working on: a document that was written almost entirely by James Madison. The delegates referred to this plan as the Virginia Plan.[16]

James Madison is considered the Father of the Constitution, yet he disagreed with this accolade. He humbly stated that this document was "not the off-spring of a single brain, but the work of many heads and many hands."

The Virginia delegates didn't believe that the Articles of Confederation could be revised. There were too many defects in the plan. The Virginia Plan called for a brand-new document to be written. Its main points were that the federal government would

- be a strong national government with the power to provide for the common defense, secure liberties, and promote the general welfare of the people.
- be organized into three separate branches (executive, legislative, and judicial). Each branch would have its own specific powers and be able to check the powers of the other branches.
- have a legislature made up of two houses that would have seats decided by a state's population.
- have a national executive that was made up of one person who would have the right to veto acts made by the legislature.
- have the power to veto laws that were passed by state legislatures.
- have the power to amend the Constitution with state approval obtained by a majority vote.[17]

For the next several weeks of the convention, the delegates passionately debated the Virginia Plan. Some of them feared that a strong central government would swallow up the states and make them powerless. They especially did not like the idea that the national government could veto laws that were passed by the state legislatures.

Another important issue was representation in the legislature. In fact, this issue became one of the hottest debate topics of the entire convention. The small states did not like the idea that the number of representatives in the legislature would be based on the size of a state's population. If this were to happen, then the small states knew they would have little say in the new government. The large states would be able to pass laws that favored only them, or so the small states feared. As Delaware delegate John Dickinson asked on June 7, "Will not these large states crush the small ones whenever they stand in the way of

John Dickinson was a delegate from Delaware. After the convention, he wrote a series of nine letters under the pseudonym of "Fabius" which was published as a pamphlet. In these letters, he encouraged the public to support the new Constitution and to vote to ratify it.

their ambitious or interested views?"[18] The small states thus wanted things to stay as they had been under the Articles of Confederation: each state should have an equal vote. The Delaware delegates even threatened to leave the convention if each state didn't have equal representation in the legislature.[19] The delegates from New Jersey were frustrated too. They said that it would be just as unfair to give more representation to large states as it would be to give more votes to a rich citizen over a poor one.[20] The small states banded together and promised that they would never agree to this part of the Virginia Plan.

On the other hand, representatives from some of the large states didn't think it was fair that 100 people in Pennsylvania (for example) would have the same say in the government as only 5 people in Rhode Island. When it came to representation in the national government, every person should be accounted for. Since the states were all of different sizes, both in geography and in population, there seemed to be no fair way to assure that the states would have equal say in the government.

The Delegates Arrive

On May 3, 1787, a stagecoach clattered through downtown Philadelphia. When it stopped in front of Mary House's boardinghouse on the corner of Fifth and Market Streets, the driver hopped down and opened the coach door. Out climbed James Madison. He was the first of the Federal Convention's delegates to arrive. He had just been in New York for the Confederation Congress. Now, here he was in Philadelphia, days early for the convention. He planned to look over his notes for the meeting and recuperate after his long journey from New York City.[21]

Ten days later, George Washington arrived from his home in Mount Vernon, Virginia, about 140 miles away. He was greeted with much fanfare. Church bells all across the city rang out. Thirteen Revolutionary War soldiers—one to represent each of the states—fired a thirteen-gun salute. In the drizzling rain, crowds of Philadelphians lined the streets to welcome General Washington to their city.[22]

Washington also planned to stay at Mrs. House's boardinghouse, but delegate Robert Morris insisted that he lodge at his home on the corner of Market and Sixth Streets. Washington graciously accepted, staying at the Morris home throughout the convention.[23]

The Federal Convention was supposed to begin on May 14, 1787, with delegates from at least seven of the thirteen states. However, on that date, delegates from only Virginia and Pennsylvania had arrived. Every day, they walked to the statehouse to see if there were enough delegates to start the meeting. Each day a few more delegates arrived. Finally, on May 25, delegates from seven states—Virginia, Pennsylvania, New York, Delaware, South Carolina, North Carolina, and New Jersey—were in attendance. The convention could officially begin.[24]

Mary House's boardinghouse

Chapter 3

A Hot and Muggy SUMMER

The weather in Philadelphia had moved from cool and rainy to hot and muggy.[1] It was a typical East Coast summer, but for the delegates inside the statehouse, the air was unusually stifling. They had decided at the beginning of the convention to keep all the doors and windows closed tight. The delegates didn't want the public to be able to spy on the proceedings.[2] This idea was all well and good when the outside temperatures were cool, but as the temperatures rose, it became another issue entirely. What made matters worse for the delegates was the clothing that was customary for the time period. Men wore high-necked long-sleeved shirts, waistcoats, and fitted wool coats all year long, regardless of the weather. Many of them even wore powdered wigs. Wearing this attire inside a hot room with no ventilation must have made the men miserable indeed.

Despite the uncomfortable conditions inside the statehouse, the delegates kept coming each morning

When people visit Independence Hall during the summer, they can experience just what it was like for the men to work in the hot and humid conditions during the summer of 1787.

In the Assembly Room in Independence Hall, the Declaration of Independence was signed. It was also here that the Constitution was debated, drafted, and signed. George Washington sat in the chair at the front of the room.

to debate the issues. Many walked from their nearby homes or boardinghouses, and some arrived by carriage. Benjamin Franklin always arrived in his customary way—carried into the statehouse in a sedan chair—since he had trouble walking.[3] When the men arrived, they took their spots at the green-cloth-covered tables in the Assembly Room. George Washington sat at the head of the room in the president's desk, and James Madison and the convention secretary sat to Washington's right.[4] Madison took detailed notes of every minute of the meeting. He wrote rapidly so that he wouldn't miss anything. He knew that what they were doing was very important, and he wanted a record of it for future generations.[5]

On Monday, June 11, 1787, the delegates gathered and continued their discussion on the issue of representation. It must have been exhausting to talk about this issue over and over again. They had been discussing it just about every day since the Virginia Plan had been introduced at the end of May.

Delegate James Wilson of Pennsylvania requested permission from Washington to take the floor. He wanted to present an idea that he felt would be a possible compromise. Wilson suggested that the representation for the legislature be based on what he called equitable representation. This representation would count every free person as one person and every slave living in the states as three-fifths of a person.

Wilson's idea was naturally intriguing to the Southern delegates. After all, their population of free people was very small. So, even though their states were large geographically, they would have little say in the lawmaking process. However, if their slaves could be counted as part of their population, then they would have more representation in the legislature.[6]

Of course, this idea seemed more than just a little ironic to some of the Northern delegates. How was it right to keep people in bondage and not treat them as people, and then turn around and count them as people to show a higher state population? Delegate Elbridge Gerry of Massachusetts (the only state at the time that outlawed slavery) took the floor. He argued that the South treated black people as property. They used slaves to do the same work that people in the North used horses and oxen to do. So, if the South wanted to count their "property" as population, then the North should get to count theirs, too.[7]

This wasn't the only time that the issue of slavery would be brought up at the convention. In the future, it would bring about even more contentious debates.

On June 15, the delegates of the small states had come together to propose their own plan, which they called the New Jersey Plan. William Paterson of New Jersey presented it.

With the New Jersey Plan, Congress

- would have the right to levy taxes.
- could tax the people based on population size, as determined by using the number of free people plus three-fifths of others.
- would have the right to regulate trade.
- would be responsible for electing the nation's executive.

Also, as part of the plan,

- the nation would have a judiciary system.
- the legislature would have only one house, not two.
- each state would be given one vote.
- a unanimous vote would be required for some items of business and a majority vote would be required for others.
- any changes made to the Constitution would have to be approved by the state legislatures with a unanimous vote.[8]

William Paterson was a delegate from New Jersey. He was a Princeton graduate, lawyer, and signer of the Declaration of Independence. At the Federal Convention, he defended the idea of states' rights and was a coauthor of the New Jersey (Paterson) Plan.

All day long on Saturday, June 16, the delegates debated the Virginia and New Jersey plans. They discussed the pros and cons of each.[9] The following Monday, the delegates were supposed to decide which of the plans they wanted to choose. But then Alexander Hamilton, a delegate from New York, asked to take the floor.

He spoke to the delegates for five hours on June 18. To many, his speech could have and should have been cut down by several hours. He explained that he wanted to introduce another plan. In Hamilton's plan:

- the executive would be appointed for life as long as he showed good behavior.
- the executive would have the power to veto any law.
- the legislature would be made up of an Assembly and a Senate; both would have power to pass all the laws.
- the states would be eliminated.
- the Senate would have sole power to declare war.

Hamilton may have had a few good ideas, but he lost any chance for support when he talked about the executive having lifetime power. The delegates weren't keen on signing up for what sounded to them like a government with another king.[10]

Hamilton's plan was never taken seriously enough to go to vote. Eventually, the New Jersey Plan was voted down.[11] It was left for the delegates to debate and revise the Virginia Plan.

It seemed clear after these weeks of intense debating that each delegate had brought to the convention his own deeply held views about how the United States government should be organized. As the debates continued day after day, tensions grew high. Sometimes tempers became so heated that some of the delegates threatened to abandon the convention altogether and go home. Eventually, the New York delegates did just that.[12] It could easily be said that the debates brought just as much heat into the statehouse as did the sweltering summer weather.

Charles Pinckney was a delegate from South Carolina. He owned seven plantations, which were operated by slave labor. This house, called the Snee Farm, was one of them. It is located near Charleston, South Carolina, and is now a national historic site.

One of the important issues under discussion was that of slavery. People were passionate about this issue, both for and against it. Northerners such as Rufus King from Massachusetts and Gouverneur Morris from Pennsylvania wholeheartedly disagreed with it.[13] They spoke about the ills that it created for the country as a whole. Delegates from the South generally had the exact opposite view. Charles Pinckney of South Carolina argued that his state could not exist without slave labor. John Rutledge went so far as to promise that the Southern states would not be part of the country if slavery were abolished.[14]

It was clear through all these heated debates that if the Constitution were ever going to be agreed upon, everyone would need to make compromises.

Franklin's Plea

During the intense debates, Benjamin Franklin would often share his wisdom. Since he had difficulty standing and walking, a fellow Pennsylvania delegate, James Wilson, would usually take the floor and read Franklin's prepared speeches for him. Franklin may have been weak physically, but his mind was as sharp as ever.

Toward the end of June, Wilson addressed the delegates with one of Franklin's speeches. In it, Franklin commented on how the convention had progressed so far. He mentioned that they had all taken time to read and learn about the successes and failures of governments in other places, but none of them had taken the time to go to their higher source of power to ask for help. He reminded them that in that very Assembly Room the Continental Congress had offered "daily prayer in this room for the divine protection," which he believed had been answered. Franklin suggested to the delegates that they would all benefit by doing the same now. We should ask "the Father of lights to illuminate our understandings," he suggested.

Roger Sherman of Connecticut seconded Franklin's motion. The group discussed it and weighed the pros and cons. However, in the end, it was decided that although it was a good idea, it simply couldn't work. A clergy member would need to be paid to offer these prayers each morning, and the Convention simply did not have the funds.[15]

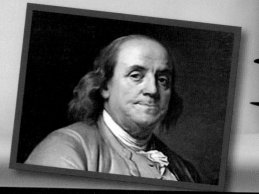

Benjamin
Franklin

Chapter 4

The Value of COMPROMISE

Both the weather in Philadelphia and the atmosphere inside the statehouse continued to be fiery throughout the end of June and early part of July. Up to this point, a variety of important decisions had been made. For one, there would be two houses in the legislature: the House of Representatives and the Senate. Senators would need to be at least 30 years old and Representatives would need to be 25. Senators would serve six-year terms and Representatives would serve two-year terms.[1]

Even though those decisions had been made, the states still had not agreed on the issue of representation. Over the Fourth of July holiday, most of the delegates took a three-day recess from the convention. A committee of eleven men stayed: their task was to find a solution to this problem. The committee included Oliver Ellsworth, Robert Yates, Gunning Bedford, William Davie, John Rutledge,

The delegates discussed and argued important matters throughout the summer of 1787.

Abraham Baldwin, Roger Sherman, William Paterson, Luther Martin, Benjamin Franklin, George Mason, and Elbridge Gerry.[2]

They were successful. The proposal they wrote became known as the Great Compromise. Of course, when the Great Compromise was presented to them on July 5, the delegates were not immediately convinced. They debated over the issues for another eleven days. Some still did not like the idea of counting slaves in the population. But if they were not counted, the Southern states would leave. Some still did not like the idea of equal votes in the Senate. But if this did not happen, then the small states would throw in the towel. There was absolutely nothing that would make *all* the states happy, so they had to compromise on many issues to give them most of what they wanted.

This was the Great Compromise that finally settled the issue of representation in the legislature:

- The House of Representatives would have representation based on population. Each state would have one representative for every 30,000 people. If a state did not have that large of a population, then they would still have at least one representative. Population would be determined by adding all the free people and three-fifths of all other persons. Direct tax would be determined for each state based on the population.
- Every state would have two senators regardless of population size.[3]

Representation wasn't, of course, the only issue that was debated at great length at the convention. The delegates still had to decide upon other important issues. For example, what power would the legislature have? How would the executive and judicial branches be organized, and what powers would they each have? How would new states that entered the Union be treated? Would it be possible to add to the Constitution later on?

First, the delegates discussed the powers that should be given to each of the three branches of government. The two-house legislature would have the power to make the laws. It would have the power to tax the people, regulate trade between the states and other nations, coin money, establish post offices, raise an army and navy, declare war, and borrow money.[4]

The delegates went on to decide the powers of the executive branch. It had already been agreed that the head of the executive branch should be one person and that this person would be called the president. It was also assumed that the first president of the United States would be George Washington.[5] He never campaigned for the position nor suggested in any way that he should be chosen. He was just so beloved by his fellow delegates and the rest of the country that he was the natural choice.

The delegates decided that the president would be the commander in chief, would have the power to make treaties (with approval by the Senate), and could either sign or veto laws that came from the legislature. The president could be removed from office by impeachment by the legislature. A person running for president had to be born in the United

George Washington became the country's first president. He had served as commander in chief of the Continental Army during the Revolutionary War and was also the president of the Constitutional Convention.

States and be at least 35 years old. In addition to a president, the executive branch would also have a vice president. The president could choose cabinet members to help him or her fulfill specific responsibilities of the office.[6]

Next, the delegates debated how the president would be elected. It was finally decided to use a special system called the Electoral College. The public would vote in a general election every four years for president. They would not be voting directly for the president, however. The electors would vote for the president, basing their votes on the will of the people they represented.[7] This system was designed as a way to prevent unscrupulous people from taking over the executive office.

The delegates discussed at length the powers of the judicial branch. This branch includes the courts. The delegates decided that the top court in the land would be called the Supreme Court. The judges in this court would be recommended by the president and confirmed by the Senate. They would serve for life. This branch would have the power to decide whether laws were fair and were written in accordance to the Constitution.[8]

Another source of debate at the convention was what to do with future states. Some suggested that the 13 original states should have more rights than any new state. Other delegates disagreed with this view. They said that the 13 states would then turn into colonizers. They couldn't treat the people of future states like second-class citizens, as the British had treated them. It was eventually agreed that any new state added would have the same rights as any other state.[9]

One of the most important parts of the Constitution is the ability for future generations to add to it, if needed. This is called the amendment process and makes the Constitution a living document. It can grow and change with time. However, the delegates were smart when they designed the amendment process. They didn't make it easy to change the Constitution. In order to add an amendment, two-thirds of both houses in the legislature would have to approve it, and then three-fourths of the states would have to ratify it. Since 1787, twenty-seven amendments have been added to the Constitution.[10]

Slavery and the Constitution

The delegates knew that if they pushed the issue of slavery too far, the union would completely dissolve. They had to come to a compromise.

The first compromise was to count slaves as three-fifths of a person. The Northern delegates did not agree with this. "Are they men? Then make them citizens and let them vote," argued Gouverneur Morris of Pennsylvania. The North finally agreed to let the slaves be counted for representation only if taxes were also computed based on population.[11]

The second compromise dealing with slavery had to do with the slave trade. The Northern delegates found the slave trade to be despicable. The Southerners claimed it was necessary for their economy. In the end, it was agreed that the slave trade could continue for another twenty years, but that was it. In the meantime, a tax would have to be paid on slaves brought into the country, too. At the time, it seemed that this compromise would slow the slave trade, but during those twenty years, approximately 170,000 people from Africa were sold as slaves in the United States.[12]

The issue of slavery definitely wasn't resolved at the Constitutional Convention. It was simply delayed. When the Civil War started in April 1861, John Adams's grandson (Charles Francis Adams) wrote in his journal, "We the children of the third and fourth generation are doomed to pay the penalties of the compromises made by the first."[13]

Charles Francis Adams

Chapter 5

Off to the STATES

The morning of September 17, 1787, was brisk in Philadelphia. In fact, throughout the entire day, the temperature never rose above 50 degrees. It was by far the chilliest day of the entire convention.[1] To the delegates, though, the weather probably didn't make the slightest bit of difference. As they made their way to the statehouse, they knew it would be the last time they would enter the hall for the Constitutional Convention. Their work was just about finished.

Over the last several weeks, the document had been drafted and revised and then drafted and revised again. Now, Gouverneur Morris—"the penman of the Constitution"—had finished the final draft.[2] It was ready for the delegates to sign.

After the men were assembled, Franklin requested that Wilson read a final speech that he had prepared. In it, he commended the men for the work they had done on the Constitution. He wrote that he knew it wasn't a perfect document, but that it was as perfect as it could be. "I doubt too whether any other

Scene at the Signing of the Constitution of the United States, painted by Howard Chandler Christy in 1940, is one of the most accurate depictions of the event. The original is 20 feet by 30 feet. It hangs in the east stairway of the House of Representatives wing of the Capitol in Washington, D.C.

convention we can obtain, may be able to make a better Constitution," he claimed. Then he requested that each of the delegates please sign their names to the document, just as he planned to do.[3]

As the president of the convention, George Washington was the first to sign. Then other delegates stood in line to affix their signatures to the Constitution. Only three of them—Elbridge Gerry, Edmund Randolph, and George Mason—refused to sign for their own individual reasons. The meeting was officially adjourned at four o'clock in the afternoon.[4]

The delegates all met that evening at the City Tavern for a celebratory dinner before they departed for home. While they dined in front of a cozy fire, the final copy of the Constitution was at the printer's.[5] John Dunlap and David Claypoole worked tirelessly late into the evening setting the type on their shop's printing press.[6] When they finished, they had copies ready for the delegates to take home to their states. Although the delegates had agreed to the Constitution, it was not yet the law of the land. It still had to be ratified by nine of the states. The opening lines of the Constitution read, "We the People of the United States . . . do ordain and establish this Constitution for the United States of America." The people had to have their say, too.

George Washington was the first to sign the Constitution.

Over the next few months, there were mixed reactions to the Constitution. Some were for it. These people were known as the Federalists. Some were against it. They were the anti-federalists. Federalists such as James Madison and Alexander Hamilton wrote essays that were published in New York newspapers.[7] These essays explained why the Articles of Confederation had failed and why this new constitution would not. The collection of 85 essays would eventually be known as the *Federalist Papers.*[8]

The anti-federalist viewpoint was heard, too. The "Centinel" essays, believed to have been written by Samuel Bryan, were published in several newspapers around the country. In these essays, the "Centinel" criticized the Constitution for taking away too many of the states' rights and making the central government too strong. He also wrote that the Constitution should have included a bill of rights to protect the rights of the people. Since it didn't have one, the anti-federalists could not endorse it.[9]

The states needed to vote on whether or not they wanted to accept, or ratify, the Constitution. On December 7, 1787, Delaware became the first state to ratify the Constitution. Pennsylvania followed just five days later. New Jersey, Georgia, Connecticut, Maryland, and South Carolina also ratified it over the next few months.[10] Massachusetts ratified it; however, it only did so on the condition that a bill of rights be added. New York and Virginia required the same thing.[11]

The ninth state to ratify the Constitution, New Hampshire, signed on June 21, 1788. A majority had been reached, and the Constitution was officially the law of the land. Shortly after, Virginia and New York ratified it too.[12]

Grand celebrations erupted in many cities throughout the country, including Philadelphia on July 4, 1788. The year before in the city, the delegates had been struggling to reach a compromise on many important issues. Now the city was filled with excitement as a big parade marched through town, speeches were given, and artillery shots were fired in salute.[13]

Eventually, all 13 states ratified the Constitution. North Carolina did so in November 1789, followed by Rhode Island on May 29, 1790.[14]

James Madison is considered the Father of the Constitution because he drafted the original Virginia Plan. Most of the Constitution originated from this document. He is also considered the Father of the Bill of Rights. This is rather ironic considering he was a Federalist and wasn't necessarily in favor of a bill of rights. Yet he knew that this first set of amendments was important to the states that had ratified the Constitution only if a bill of rights were added.

Sometime in 1788, Madison sat down to start drafting the amendments. He spent a great deal of time researching important historical documents, just as he had done when he drafted the Virginia Plan. He studied the English Bill of Rights, the Magna Carta, and the Virginia Declaration of Rights.

Congress had planned to meet in 1789. By that time, Madison had completed a list of seventeen rights for Congress to consider. The delegates debated these rights and approved a list of twelve amendments to send to the states. The states ratified all but two of them.[15] With this ratification, the Bill of Rights became the first ten amendments to the

The delegates made sure that the people could add specific rights to the Constitution through an amendment process. The first ten amendments added to the Constitution are called the Bill of Rights.

Constitution. They specifically explain the rights of individuals in the United States. They include such things as freedom of religion, freedom of speech, freedom to assemble, and freedom of the press. With the passing of the Bill of Rights, the young nation showed that its Constitution was indeed a living document that could grow with the needs of the people.

The Constitution of the United States is considered one of the most important documents in both United States and world history. It is the longest surviving charter on government in the history of the world. It has inspired many other nations to establish their own governments on similar principles. The men who framed the Constitution were not perfect. The document they created was not perfect. But it has stood the test of time and has remained the supreme law of the land even through the country's darkest hours.

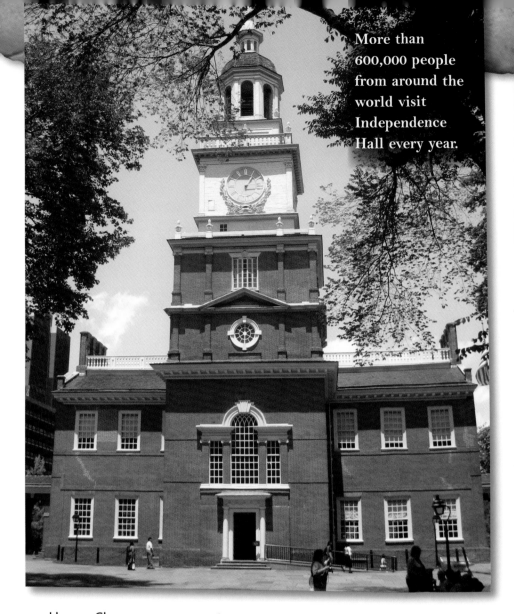

More than 600,000 people from around the world visit Independence Hall every year.

Henry Clay, a senator and representative from Kentucky who also served as secretary of state, said this in 1850: "The Constitution of the United States was made not merely for the generation that then existed, but for posterity—unlimited, undefined, endless, perpetual posterity."[16]

The Constitution is indeed a living document that continues to defend our freedoms and shape our country's history.

A Rising Sun

As the last of the delegates were signing the Constitution on September 17, 1787, Benjamin Franklin looked toward the chair in which Washington had been sitting for the entire convention. On top of the chair was a carving of the sun. He remarked to a few of the delegates who were standing near him that artists often struggle to distinguish in their artwork between a rising and a setting sun. He said that throughout the convention, he would often look at this sun and wonder if it was rising or setting on their young nation. "Now at length, I have the happiness to know that it is a rising and not a setting sun," he concluded as he watched the last delegate sign his name to the document.[17]

Washington's chair remains on display in Independence Hall. The Assembly Room is set up to look just as it did in the 1780s.

The carving on Washington's chair

TIMELINE

1775   George Washington is elected as commander in chief of the Continental army.

1776   The Declaration of Independence is adopted at the Pennsylvania State House.

1777   The stars and stripes are chosen as the United States flag design.

1781   The Articles of Confederation are ratified in March. Cornwallis surrenders to Washington at Yorktown in October.

1783   The Treaty of Paris, officially ending the Revolutionary War, is signed.

1786   Regulators begin marching on courthouses in Massachusetts in the fall.

1787   In Springfield, Massachusetts, a group of Regulators led by Daniel Shays and a government militia led by General William Shepard clash during Shays' Rebellion (January 25). On May 25, the first official day of the Constitutional Convention, George Washington is chosen as president. Edmund Randolph of Virginia proposes the Virginia Plan and Charles Pinckney propose his plan on May 29. On June 11, James Wilson of Pennsylvania suggests the three-fifths compromise. Within a week, William Paterson of New Jersey proposes the New Jersey Plan, and Alexander Hamilton of New York proposes the Hamilton Plan. The Great Compromise is written and presented July 2–5. The U.S. Constitution is signed September 17. Delaware ratifies the Constitution December 7, becoming the first state to do so. It is followed by Pennsylvania and New Jersey.

1788   Georgia, Connecticut, Massachusetts, Maryland, and South Carolina sign the Constitution. When New Hampshire ratifies the Constitution June 21, it is the ninth state to do so, officially making the Constitution the law of the land.

1789   In September, Congress approves twelve amendments to be sent to the states for ratification.

1790   Rhode Island ratifies the Constitution.

1791   Virginia becomes the tenth of fourteen states to approve ten of the twelve amendments proposed by Congress. The Bill of Rights becomes part of the Constitution.

Chapter 1

1. Charles Phillips, "A Day to Remember: January 25, 1787: Shays' Rebellion Gets Bloody," *American History Magazine,* February 2007, pp. 17–18.
2. David O. Stewart, *The Summer of 1787: The Men Who Invented the Constitution* (New York: Simon & Schuster, 2007), pp. 26–27.
3. *Shays' Rebellion & the Making of a Nation,* "Daniel Shays," Springfield Technical Community College, http://shaysrebellion.stcc.edu/shaysapp/person.do?shortName=daniel_shays
4. *Shays' Rebellion & the Making of a Nation,* "A Bloody Encounter," http://shaysrebellion.stcc.edu/shaysapp/scene.do?shortName=Arsenal
5. Phillips.
6. *Shays' Rebellion & the Making of a Nation,* "Petition and Protest," http://shaysrebellion.stcc.edu/shaysapp/scene.do?shortName=Petition
7. *Shays' Rebellion & the Making of a Nation,* "Abigail Adams," http://shaysrebellion.stcc.edu/shaysapp/person.do?shortName=abigail_adams
8. Phillips.
9. *Shays' Rebellion & the Making of a Nation,* "A Bloody Encounter."
10. Phillips.
11. American Memory, "America During the Age of Revolution, 1776–1789," The Library of Congress, http://memory.loc.gov/ammem/collections/continental/timeline2f.html
12. Stewart, p. 34.
13. Ibid., p. 38.
14. *The Charters of Freedom,* "A More Perfect Union: The Creation of the U.S. Constitution," The U.S. National Archives & Records Administration, http://www.archives.gov/exhibits/charters/constitution_history.html
15. American Memory, "Identifying Defects in the Confederation," The Library of Congress, http://memory.loc.gov/ammem/collections/continental/defects.html

Chapter 2

1. David O. Stewart, *The Summer of 1787: The Men Who Invented the Constitution* (New York: Simon & Schuster, 2007), p. 62.
2. *The Charters of Freedom,* "A More Perfect Union: The Creation of the U.S. Constitution," The U.S. National Archives & Records Administration, http://www.archives.gov/exhibits/charters/constitution_history.html
3. "Madison Debates, May 25, 1787," Avalon Project: Documents in Law, History, and Diplomacy; Yale Law School, Lillian Goldman Law Library, http://avalon.law.yale.edu/18th_century/debates_514525.asp.
4. "A More Perfect Union: The Creation of the U.S. Constitution."
5. Ibid.
6. "Independence Hall, National Historical Park, Pennsylvania," National Park Service, http://www.nps.gov/inde/independence-hall-1.htm
7. Ibid.
8. Ibid.
9. Ibid.
10. Stewart, p. 38.
11. "Madison Debates, May 25, 1787."
12. Ibid.
13. Ibid.
14. Ibid.
15. "Madison Debates, May 29, 1787," http://avalon.law.yale.edu/18th_century/debates_528.asp
16. Ibid.
17. Ibid.
18. "Madison Debates, June 8, 1787," http://avalon.law.yale.edu/18th_century/debates_608.asp
19. Stewart, pp. 75–76.
20. "Madison Debates, June 8, 1787."
21. Stewart, pp. 42–43.
22. Stewart, pp. 44–45.
23. "Sunday, May 13, 1787: Washington Arrives in Philadelphia." *Independence.* National Historical Park Pennsylvania, http://www.nps.gov/inde/historyculture/washington-philadelphia.htm
24. "Monday, May 14, 1787–Thursday, May 24, 1787." *Independence.* National Historical Park Pennsylvania, http://www.nps.gov/inde/historyculture/quorum-convention.htm

Chapter 3

1. *The Charters of Freedom,* "A More Perfect Union: The Creation of the U.S. Constitution," The U.S. National Archives & Records Administration, http://www.archives.gov/exhibits/charters/constitution_history.html
2. *Creating the United States,* "Setting for the Creation of the Federal Constitution," http://myloc.gov/Exhibitions/creatingtheus/Constitution/RoadtotheConstitution/ExhibitObjects/SettingforCreationofFederalConstitution.aspx
3. David O. Stewart, *The Summer of 1787: The Men Who Invented the Constitution* (New York: Simon & Schuster, 2007), p. 45.
4. Ibid., p. 76.
5. *The Charters of Freedom.*

6. Stewart, pp. 90–94.
7. "Madison Debates, June 11, 1787," Avalon Project: Documents in Law, History, and Diplomacy; Yale Law School, Lillian Goldman Law Library, http://avalon.law.yale.edu/18th_century/debates_611.asp
8. "Madison Debates, June 15, 1787," http://avalon.law.yale.edu/18th_century/debates_615.asp
9. "Madison Debates, June 16, 1787," http://avalon.law.yale.edu/18th_century/debates_616.asp
10. "Madison Debates, June 18, 1787," http://avalon.law.yale.edu/18th_century/debates_618.asp
11. *The Charters of Freedom.*
12. Stewart, p. 188.
13. David Reynolds, *America, Empire of Liberty* (New York: Basic Books, 2009), p. 60.
14. "Madison Debates, August 21, 1787," http://avalon.law.yale.edu/18th_century/debates_821.asp, and "Madison Debates, August 22, 1787," http://avalon.law.yale.edu/18th_century/debates_822.asp
15. "Madison Debates, June 28, 1787," http://avalon.law.yale.edu/18th_century/debates_628.asp

Chapter 4

1. *The Charters of Freedom,* The Constitution of the United States, transcript, http://www.archives.gov/exhibits/charters/constitution_transcript.html
2. "Madison Debates, July 2, 1787," Avalon Project: Documents in Law, History, and Diplomacy; Yale Law School, Lillian Goldman Law Library, http://avalon.law.yale.edu/18th_century/debates_702.asp
3. The Constitution of the United States.
4. Ibid.
5. David O. Stewart, *The Summer of 1787: The Men Who Invented the Constitution* (New York: Simon & Schuster, 2007). pp. 167–168.
6. The Constitution of the United States.
7. George Brown Tindall, *America, A Narrative History* (New York: W. W. Norton Company, 1999), p. 317.
8. The Constitution of the United States.
9. Stewart, p. 151.
10. The Constitution of the United States.
11. "Madison Debates, August 8, 1787," http://avalon.law.yale.edu/18th_century/debates_808.asp
12. Stewart, p. 219.

13. Doris Kearns Goodwin, *Team of Rivals: The Political Genius of Abraham Lincoln* (New York: Simon & Schuster, 2005), p. 352.

Chapter 5

1. David O. Stewart, *The Summer of 1787: The Men Who Invented the Constitution* (New York: Simon & Schuster, 2007), p. 257.
2. "America During the Age of Revolution, 1776–1789," The Library of Congress, http://memory.loc.gov/ammem/collections/continental/timeline2f.html
3. "Madison Debates, September 17, 1787," Avalon Project: Documents in Law, History, and Diplomacy; Yale Law School, Lillian Goldman Law Library, http://avalon.law.yale.edu/18th_century/debates_917.asp
4. Ibid.
5. Stewart, p. 257.
6. "The Official Edition of the Constitution printed by Dunlap & Claypoole," Historical Society of Pennsylvania, http://hsp.org/history-online/exhibits/constitution-on-display/the-official-edition-of-the-constitution-printed-by-dunlap-claypoole
7. *The Charters of Freedom:* "A More Perfect Union: The Creation of the U.S. Constitution," The U.S. National Archives & Records Administration, http://www.archives.gov/exhibits/charters/constitution_history.html
8. Ibid.
9. Ibid.
10. George Brown Tindall, *America, A Narrative History* (New York: W. W. Norton Company, 1999), p. 322.
11. *The Charters of Freedom.*
12. Tindall, p. 322.
13. Stewart, pp. 260–263.
14. Tindall, p. 322.
15. *Primary Documents in American History:* The Bill of Rights, The Library of Congress, http://www.loc.gov/rr/program/bib/ourdocs/billofrights.html
16. "Henry Clay Biographical Sketch," Ashland, The Henry Clay Estate, http://www.henryclay.org/henry-clay/attorney/
17. "Madison Debates, September 17, 1787," http://avalon.law.yale.edu/18th_century/debates_917.asp

Books

Allen, Kathy. *The U.S. Constitution.* Mankato, MN: Capstone Press, 2006.

Cheney, Lynn. *We the People: The Story of Our Constitution.* New York: Simon & Schuster Children's Publishing, 2008.

Leavitt, Amie Jane. *The Bill of Rights* (My Guide to the Constitution). Hockessin, DE: Mitchell Lane Publishers, 2012.

———. *The Bill of Rights in Translation: What It Really Means.* Mankato, MN: Capstone Press, 2008.

Taylor-Butler, Christine. *The Constitution of the United States.* New York: Children's Press (Scholastic), 2008.

Travis, Cathy. *Constitution Translated for Kids.* Austin, Texas: Synergy Books, 2006.

Works Consulted

The Charters of Freedom: "The U.S. Constitution." The U.S. National Archives & Records Administration. http://www.archives.gov/exhibits/charters/constitution_history.html

"Documents from the Continental Congress and the Constitutional Convention, 1774–1789." The Library of Congress. http://memory.loc.gov/ammem/collections/continental/index.html

"Madison Debates." Avalon Project: Documents in Law, History, and Diplomacy. Yale Law School. Lillian Goldman Law Library. http://avalon.law.yale.edu/subject_menus/debcont.asp

"Official Edition of the Constitution Printed by Dunlap & Claypoole." Historical Society of Pennsylvania. http://hsp.org/history-online/exhibits/constitution-on-display/the-official-edition-of-the-constitution-printed-by-dunlap-claypoole

Phillips, Charles. "A Day to Remember: January 25, 1787: Shays' Rebellion Gets Bloody." *American History Magazine,* February 2007.

Primary Documents in American History: "The Bill of Rights." The Library of Congress. http://www.loc.gov/rr/program/bib/ourdocs/billofrights.html

Shays' Rebellion & the Making of a Nation. Springfield Technical Community College. http://shaysrebellion.stcc.edu/index.html

Stewart, David O. *The Summer of 1787: The Men Who Invented the Constitution.* New York: Simon & Schuster, 2007.

Tindall, George Brown. *America, A Narrative History.* New York: W. W. Norton Company, 1999.

On the Internet

Constitution Center
    http://constitutioncenter.org/
The Library of Congress
    http://www.loc.gov/index.html
The U.S. National Archives & Records Administration
    http://www.archives.gov

adjourn—To end or close a meeting.

ambassador—A country's official representative to a foreign country.

amendment—An official change or addition.

Bill of Rights—The first ten amendments to the Constitution.

cabinet—A group of advisers.

compromise—A settlement of differences between people, where each side gives up some demands in order to reach an agreement.

constitution—The official framework of a government.

contentious—Eager to argue or fight.

endorse—To declare one's approval of a person, product, or action.

equitable—Being fair or just.

executive—Related to carrying out or enforcing laws. The executive branch of government is headed by a president (for a nation) or a governor (for a state).

financier—A person who provides money for a business or project.

gout—An extremely painful disease of the joints.

impeachment—The legal process used to remove a person from office because of misconduct.

judicial—Relating to courts or judges. The judicial branch of the U.S. government is headed by the Supreme Court.

legislative—Having the power to create laws. The legislative branch of the U.S. government consists of the Senate and the House of Representatives; together, these two bodies form the U.S. Congress.

levy—The declaration and collection of taxes.

posterity—Future generations.

ratify—To give official approval.

Regulator—One of the followers of Daniel Shays, who wanted to bring reform to the U.S. government.

unanimously—By total agreement.

unscrupulous—Lacking moral values and principles.

veteran—A person who has served in the military.

veto—To stop a bill from becoming a law after a legislature has already approved it.

INDEX

Adams, John   14, 33

amendment process   32

Articles of Confederation   6, 10, 11, 15–18, 19, 37

Assembly Room   15, 22

Baldwin, Abraham   30

Bedford, Gunning   28

Bill of Rights   37, 38–39

Clay, Henry   40

Confederation Congress   11, 19

Congress   6, 10, 11, 15, 19, 24, 27, 38

Connecticut   27, 38

Continental Army   15, 19

Continental Congress   15, 19, 27

Davie, William   28

Declaration of Independence   10, 14–15, 19, 22, 24

Delaware   17–18, 38

Dickinson, John   17–18

Electoral College   32

Ellsworth, Oliver   28

executive branch   30, 31–32

Federal Convention (Constitutional Convention)   10, 12–20, 22–25, 27–28, 30, 32–34, 36, 41

Federalist Papers   37

Franklin, Benjamin   12, 13, 19, 22, 27, 30, 34, 36, 41

Georgia   38

Gerry, Elbridge   12, 23, 30, 36

Great Compromise   30

Hamilton, Alexander   10, 12–13, 25, 37

Hamilton Plan   25

Hancock, John   9

House, Mary   19

House of Representatives   28, 30

Independence Hall (Pennsylvania State House)   10, 12, 22, 41

Jefferson, Thomas   14

judicial branch   30, 32

King, Rufus   26

legislature   17–18, 23–25, 28, 30–32 (*and see* Congress)

Madison, James   10, 12, 13, 16, 22, 37, 38

Martin, Luther   12, 30

Maryland   12, 38

Mason, George   30, 36

Massachusetts   4, 7–10, 12, 23, 26, 38

Morris, Gouverneur   12, 26, 33, 34

Morris, Robert   15, 19

New Jersey   18, 23–25, 38

New Jersey Plan   23–25

New York   12, 25, 37–38

North Carolina   38

Paterson, William   23–24, 30

Pennsylvania   10, 12, 15, 18, 23, 26–27, 33, 38

Pennsylvania State House   *see* Independence Hall

Philadelphia, Pennsylvania   10, 12, 20, 28, 34, 38, 40

Pinckney, Charles   26

Randolph, Edmund J.   16, 36

Regulators   4, 5, 8–9, 12

representatives   17–18, 28, 30

Revolutionary War   4, 6, 7, 8, 10, 11, 15, 19, 31

Rhode Island   10, 18, 38

Rutledge, John   15, 26, 28

senators   28, 30

Shays, Daniel   4, 5, 6–10

Shepard, William   9

Sherman, Roger   27, 30

slavery   24, 26, 33

South Carolina   15, 26, 38

Springfield, Massachusetts   4, 6

Virginia   12, 16–18, 23, 25, 38

Virginia Plan   16–18, 23, 25, 38

Washington, George   10, 12, 15, 19, 22–23, 31, 36–37, 41

Wilson, James   13, 23, 27, 34

Yates, Robert   28

ABOUT THE
AUTHOR

Amie Jane Leavitt is an accomplished author, researcher, and photographer. She graduated from Brigham Young University as an education major and has since taught all subjects and grade levels in both private and public schools. She is an adventurer who loves to travel the globe in search of interesting story ideas and beautiful places to capture in photos. Leavitt has written more than fifty books for kids, has contributed to online and print media, and has worked as a consultant, writer, and editor for numerous educational publishing and assessment companies. She has always had a great love for American history. One of her favorite memories is the first time she ever saw the original copy of the Constitution in the National Archives when she was a senior in high school. Since then, Leavitt has had the opportunity to visit many of our country's historic sites and has spent countless hours researching history-related topics for her various projects. To check out a listing of her current projects and published works, visit www.amiejaneleavitt.com.